Fated Mate Surprise Daddy

Fated Mates Saga, Volume 1

Luna Rains

Published by JL Lam Publishing, 2024.

FATED MATE SURPRISE DADDY

First edition. April 14, 2024.

ISBN: 979-8224472796

Written by Luna Rains.

Also by Luna Rains

Fated Mates Saga
Fated Mate Surprise Daddy
Fated Mate Triplets Daddy

Watch for more at https://lunarains.com.

Table of Contents

To my beloved husband, whose unwavering support, endless encouragement, and steadfast belief in me have been the guiding light throughout my journey. Your love is the foundation upon which I build my dreams.

Prologue

"Marie," A deep voice called my name, it was like an intimate caress that washed over my body.

I turned around to see the gorgeous man from inside standing before me. He was breathtaking with green eyes that were almost electric, jet-black hair, and beard. The dark maroon shirt he was wearing barely covered his muscular chest.

I licked my lips. He took three steps toward me, grabbed my face in his hands and kissed me passionately.

The world exploded around me. I gripped his shirt and held on for dear life as the electricity shot through my body.

"Damn, Dre!" Someone yelled behind us. He pulled away breathlessly. He leaned his forehead against mine and gazed into my eyes.

He didn't speak, his hands went down to my hips, and he picked me up. My legs instinctively went around him, and he carried me to a dark alley while still kissing me.

He pushed me against a wall, his hands and mouth exploring my body. He reached down into my top and pulled a breast out, his mouth finding my nipple.

I moaned; his warm mouth felt so good but when he included his tongue I nearly screamed. He chuckled.

His hands went down to my skirt and pulled it the rest of the way up my hips, then his fingers found my warm, dripping wet center, I leaned my head back and shuddered. His fingers entered me slowly, all the while his mouth was still working on my nipple. I moaned loudly as he pushed them in and out of me.

I ground my hips against him, my panties were soaked. I ran my palms down his back, loving the way his muscles moved under my hands.

His mouth found mine again.

His fingers left my clit and I could feel him moving to pull his cock out of his pants. I couldn't think of anything else but his hard shaft inside me.

Thunder sounded above us, and I heard his zipper go down. I pulled back from the kiss, and he looked into my eyes as he entered me.

I drew in a breath as his cock filled me.

He started to rock his hips. His balls slapped against my ass. I cried out in pleasure. He just rocked into me harder.

I called his name; he leaned his head down and bit my neck.

I let out a long, deep moan, his cock grew inside me. The sensations that were ripping through my body sped up and heightened.

His hands went under my ass, and he lifted me.

I wrapped my feet around his back as he moved. His thrusts were hard and fast.

The electricity between us was causing me to see stars. I kissed his neck and bit his shoulder. He growled and his pace sped up.

He pulled out abruptly and turned me around, my hands braced against the wall. He pushed my skirt up to my waist and positioned himself behind me.

I was so wet, I was dripping. He thrust into me hard, pausing just for a moment to let me adjust.

He moved his hands up my sides and gripped my breasts. I moaned and pushed back against him.

He continued to move his hands up my body until they found my hair. He pulled my head back; my hands left the wall and went to his arms.

He started to thrust in and out of me, my legs grew weak, and my breathing grew shallow.

His movements were steady and controlled. His mouth found my ear and he whispered, "Come for me, Marie."

I was on the brink, my body shaking. He kissed my neck and moaned, sending me over the edge.

I screamed, my body shaking violently. He growled and pushed his cock in hard, filling me completely. His hand moved my hair away from my neck and he bit down gently.

I collapsed against the wall. He pulled out gently. The sensation of him leaving my body was overwhelming. His hands caressed my bottom. I turned around and kissed him.

When we both pulled away, I reeled back and tried to slap him across the face.

"How dare you?"

He chuckled, as he grabbed my wrist. He held my hand away before he kissed my palm softly.

"You're mine, Marie."

Marie — Earlier that same day

"We are going to have the best night ever." My little sister, Selena gushed as she squeezed my arm.

"The Santiago trio is out on the prowl," Drake, Selena's best friend, teased. "The warlocks of West Haven should be scared."

"All warlocks should be scared, not just the ones in town." My older sister, Esmerelda purred as she walked into the room. She was breathtaking in a mini skirt and crop top; the same thing Selena and I were wearing. Her dark brown hair fell in waves down her back, just like mine and Selena's.

The three of us looked more like triplets, many people couldn't tell us apart. It didn't help that I was fourteen months younger than Esmerelda and fourteen months older than Selena though. I got why it was confusing.

"Most of them are extremely intimidated by the three of you." Drake chuckled.

"We're harmless," Selena giggled.

"Says the girl who turned a man into a pig after he wouldn't leave you alone."

"He identifies better with a pig," She replied batting her eyelashes. "And I turned him back into the annoying human he is."

"Only because I made you," Esmerelda giggled as she raised an eyebrow.

Selena rolled her eyes and finished putting her lipstick on. When she finished, she stood up and looked around at the three of us.

"Are we ready to go?"

"I've been ready." I teased.

"It's really not fair that Marie doesn't even have to try, and she looks like she did," Selena whined.

Esmerelda chuckled before she led us outside of the house.

"Be good tonight," My father, Ricardo Santiago, called as he walked out of the garage. If you were just passing by our little ranch house in the middle of the subdivision, you'd never guess that the man outside mowing the yard was one of the most powerful warlocks in the country. He really just looked like your average gym bro, a former football player.

My mother, Eva Santiago, walked up beside him, a glass of wine in her hand as she smiled at us.

"Don't be good tonight," she giggled. "Go out and make memories."

My mother looked like your average yoga mom. She had an amazing body for her age, most people thought she was our sister. She shared the same dark hair, dark eyes, and dark complexion that we did. She was one of the most powerful witches in the country, but you'd think all she cared about was wine, Starbucks, and yoga. We definitely blended with the rest of the world easily.

"Drake, call me if you need to," My father replied as he shook his head. We loaded into Drake's Jeep and made our way to the first bar on Selena's list. She wanted to go to two human bars and then the last one would be the only supernatural bar within fifty miles. That's where our friends would be meeting us.

The night was pretty uneventful only because I'm more of a loner and can only take so much people time. Selena and Esmerelda relished the chaos and meeting new people.

They were so adventurous, and I would rather stay locked in my bedroom with a good book. They didn't allow that to happen at all.

The human bars were disgusting. The men in there were entitled pigs. I laughed to myself at the thought of Selena turning them all into pigs.

We arrived at the supernatural bar, and I breathed a sigh of relief. Selena ordered us shots and drinks before we found a table to sit at.

"I will not be sitting long but I need to take a second to recharge," She smiled.

"Drink some water too." Esmerelda directed.

"I'm fine." Selena waved her off.

My sisters were on the dance floor within minutes. Drake moved next to me.

"There are about twenty men in here dying to talk to you."

"I don't see any of them trying."

"You're intimidating."

"How?"

"I'm not saying it's a bad thing, because it's not. It's obvious that you are confident and mature, that's intimidating to the men who are not. Don't change who you are."

I nodded my head and looked back at Drake. He was a handsome blonde, with bright blue eyes. He looked like he belonged on the cover of every young adult romance book about high school quarterbacks.

He followed Selena around like a puppy dog.

"When are you going to ask my sister out?"

"She's not interested."

"I don't know how she's not."

"She's not in a place to be interested. Does that make more sense?"

"I guess so." I nodded. Selena was still young and immature. She's always been curious about everything. She never stays with a guy for more than a few dates.

"She says she's looking for the man that rocks her world the second they lock eyes. That's obviously not me."

"She reads too many romance novels." I laughed. "It doesn't happen like that as far as I know."

"I guess it depends on the person. For some people, it's a slow burn and for others it's immediate."

"Maybe." I shrugged. "I still think you should say something to her."

"Advice from the woman who has sworn off love. I don't know if I should be flattered or offended."

"I haven't sworn off love," I argued with a laugh. "I've just sworn off idiots."

Drake chuckled and nodded his head.

I felt a wave of warmth run over my body. Tingles and goosebumps raced up my arms and I felt as though someone was looking at me.

I immediately turned in the direction I thought the feeling was coming from. It was the front door but there was nothing or no one there.

"Drake, I just got a really weird feeling. Did you get it too?"

"What type of feeling?"

"Like goosebumps and tingles. I felt like someone was watching me."

"Weird." He shook his head and looked around. "You're more in tune with energy than I am. Do you think someone with dark magic walked in?"

"No, that feels different." I sighed as I continued to look around. "It doesn't feel wrong. It feels safe and...right? Maybe."

I shook my head and tried to clear the thoughts out. I closed my eyes, inhaled, and exhaled and tried to calm the energy around me and inside of me.

I could feel something there. Something safe and magnetic, but it was just a blur of green and blue.

"I'll stay close, just in case." He stated his eyes were glued to Selena and Esmerelda as they danced with random men on the dance floor.

I felt a soft breath against my cheek as I turned toward it there was no one there. My eyes locked with a gorgeous man in a maroon shirt. His jade-green eyes pulled me in.

It was as if the entire room disappeared around us and I was yanked into him. I was standing in front of him.

Andrei.

The whisper of the man's name gave me pause, as I closed my eyes. When I opened them, I was back in my chair in the bar.

How did I know this man's name?

"Drake, I think I need to go outside for some air."

He nodded. I stood up, not looking around for the man again. I focused straight ahead of me and on the exit sign.

What a strange interaction and feeling. I needed to get outside into the fresh air and clear my head. My body felt as though it were on fire. It was as if I was being tugged in a different direction but the further, I made it to the door it, the louder my body screamed to stop.

My breathing quickened until I finally was outside of the bar. The cool night air filled my lungs, and I felt a sense of peace wash over me.

What in the hell was that? Was that a panic attack?

"Marie," I wouldn't turn around. I knew it was that man behind me.

How did he know my name?

Andrei

"Dre, I need to unwind tonight." My best friend, Matias interjected.

"Me too," I growled.

"My entire body hurts."

We had an intense training session. My father is the Alpha of the Bloodfang pack. He is training me to take over for him when the time comes.

Our pack is the best of the best. We've long been former military, special forces, or precise in the art of military and security. Matias will be my Beta.

The last few years my father has put us through rigorous training. A typical day consists of a ten-mile run, followed my whatever martial art is on the schedule for the day, followed by combat training. After combat, we go through mindfulness exercises. We lift weights daily and then we're in a classroom learning how to be the perfect weapon and soldier.

It's the end of the week and the one night we're allowed to rest and recharge. Originally, we're from Missouri. My father had sent Matias and I to a training facility in Massachusetts.

The location gave us secrecy, but it also gave us access to all types of supernaturals. There was a committee of all supernaturals that had formed after there were a lot of random killings of our people. That committee built this training facility so they could form a team of soldiers to fight against those trying to harm us.

It was an eye-opening experience as this was my first time around anyone that wasn't a werewolf.

"The Haven is the only bar you're allowed to go to," Lyle, one of the werewolf instructors growled as he walked by.

"Why's that?"

"It's a supernatural beings bar. No human bars allowed."

"I don't want to be around a human anyway," I replied with a roll of my eyes.

Matias chuckled and the two of us made our way out of the barracks and to my truck.

"I wonder why he specified that we can't go to a human bar."

"They're probably afraid we'll eat someone," I joked.

"I want to eat someone, but not in that way." Matias laughed at his own joke.

"I'm sure there will be plenty of female wolves there for you to do exactly that."

"I hope so," He replied as he rubbed his hands together.

Twenty minutes later we were at the bar. It was late and most people had been drinking for a while. As soon as we walked in, I smelled the most amazing scent of lavender and vanilla.

"Our mate is here." My wolf Indrik growled as he began pacing in my head. *"She's here right now."*

"Mate? What are you talking about?"

"Our mate is here. I don't feel her wolf, but I feel her."

"How is that possible?"

"I don't know. Find her now."

I felt as though I was going to crawl out of my skin. The smell was making me feel as though I needed to rush to this woman and keep her safe. I needed to claim her as mine.

I look around the room, scanning to see if I could find my mate. The lore says that I will smell a special scent at first, but when our eyes lock, I will know she's my mate.

I see nothing. I feel pulled to another part of the bar and I slowly make my way to the middle of the room.

A wave of heat washed over me. Indrik growled and then let out a howl just as my eyes land on an angel wearing a short black leather skirt with a red crop top, and black knee-high boots.

My body instantly responds to the sight of her toned and tanned body, her curves. My eyes make their way up her body, seeing her pouty, full red lips, and then I lock onto her amber-colored eyes.

Indrik lets out another howl. Suddenly, she's right in front of me. I lean into her ear.

"Marie."

The name falls out of my mouth as if I said it a million times. Just as quickly as I say her name, she is ripped away from me.

Indrik howls and growls, he's clawing to get out.

I'm still standing across the room and she's back to sitting at a table with a man who's paying no attention to her and drooling over two women on the dance floor.

She stood up and scurries out of the bar and I followed.

"Marie," I breathed when I come up behind her. She turns around and those amber eyes lock onto mine again. I take three steps and pull her into a kiss.

The world explodes around me. I don't know what's happening, but I can feel that I will die for this woman, that she is mine.

Marie

"You're mine, Marie." His voice washed over me, and I closed my eyes. The sound caused tingles to shoot up my spine.

I looked back at him in shock. The audacity of this man to tell me I'm his.

"No, I'm not."

"But you are. I marked you."

"Marked me? What?" I gasped as I took a step back from him.

"Why don't I feel your wolf?"

"Wolf?" I repeated.

"My wolf doesn't feel your wolf, why is that?"

"I'm not a wolf. I'm a witch. I'm a Santiago witch."

"A witch? That's not possible."

"I assure you that I am," I snapped. I jerked my head to the side, and he flew in the direction I'd moved.

He growled, stood up, and dusted himself off as he looked back at me in shock. He walked around me slowly as if he was sizing me up.

I turned on my heel and walked off.

"Everything the lore says just happened."

"I don't know what you're talking about."

"You felt it too. You feel drawn to me, pulled to me by an invisible thread and you don't know why, right?"

I turned around, my gaze flitting up to his. I nodded.

"Can I...can we go somewhere and talk?"

I shook my head. I crossed my arms in front of my chest. "I'm not going anywhere with you."

"You just went in an alley with me alone." He chuckled.

"You didn't give me a choice."

"Listen, you can say whatever you want because you're embarrassed but you were kissing me back and you definitely got off with me."

I didn't reply, just narrowed my eyes at him. He wasn't wrong.

"I don't know what's happening or why." He spoke. "But I know that you're my mate. My wolf told me."

"Your wolf talks to you?" I snapped. "Great, I found a crazy person."

"It's normal for your wolf to talk to you."

"I wouldn't know."

"It's really hard for me not to kiss you right now." He growled as he took a step forward.

I exhaled. I was having the same thoughts. I felt as though I was being pulled into him and I was fighting it with everything I had in me.

"What's stopping you?"

He moved toward me and kissed me again. My knees buckled this time.

"Go to my truck with me," He breathed in my ear. It was like I was under a spell. His fingers laced through mine.

We were at a black pickup truck. He opened the door and started to help me into the passenger seat. I shook my head and moved to the back. He grinned as he followed behind me.

As soon as the door shut, he kissed me hungrily. He pulled me into his lap, his hand going to my face possessively.

I couldn't believe I was doing this, but I couldn't stop myself either. The way he touched me, the way he kissed me, it was like nothing else mattered. Every inch of me was alive with sensation and all I wanted was more.

His hand slid down my body, tracing the curve of my waist before settling on my thigh. He pulled me closer, and I could feel his arousal pressing against my core. A moan escaped my lips, and he took it as an invitation to deepen the kiss.

I lost myself in him completely. I wanted him more than anything I had ever wanted before. His hands roamed freely over my body, setting me alight with each touch. And then suddenly, it was too much.

I pulled away, gasping for air, and tried to regain my composure.

"What's wrong?"

"I need your pants off so I can feel your cock inside me now."

He grinned back at me smugly before removing his pants. He pulled me back into him, placing me on his lap.

I moved my panties to the side and guided him inside me. I stilled for a minute as his girth filled me.

I moaned and threw my head back. He kissed my throat and thrust up into me.

He kissed my lips and grabbed my head, forcing my gaze back to his.

"Look at me," he ordered.

I forced my eyes open and did as he said. He moved inside me more forcefully, his lips returning to mine. I wrapped my legs around his thighs as best as I could in the confining space, pulling him closer to me. He grunted into the kiss as he moved faster.

I gripped the back of his head as he ground his hips against me. I felt a build-up of pressure deep within me. I was so close.

"Harder," I moaned as I threw my head back.

He did as I asked and thrust into me repeatedly. His hand cupped my face, and he kissed me deeply as he fucked me.

I wanted him even more. All I could think about was him and his hard cock and the thrill of being with him.

I tried to move my hips to meet him thrust for thrust, but it was hard to get the movement. He pressed me down with his hips and fucked me harder.

I screamed loudly as I came. He thrust into me a few more times before he gripped my hips and thrust into me almost violently. His hot release filling me.

He kissed me gently. I stared into his deep green eyes, lost in them. I wrapped my arms around his neck and kissed him back.

Andrei

"I need to get back in the bar. My sisters will be looking for me."

"My friend will be looking for me," I replied.

As soon as she climbed off my lap it felt as though I were empty.

I pulled my pants on and then climbed out of the truck. I helped her out. My fingers stayed laced with hers.

We walked back into the bar together. Matias was at the bar talking to a redheaded wolf, he cocked an eyebrow in surprise as he looked back at me.

"Who's that?" He asked via our pack mind link.

"My mate."

"Holy shit."

"My sisters are over here." She tugged me to a small group of women wearing the same clothing as her.

"Marie, where have you been?" One of them asked.

"I met someone." "He's a wolf, Marie."

"I'm her mate."

"That's not a thing," The blonde man at the table chuckled.

"It can be if the Moon Goddess says it is." One of the women said.

"I've never heard of that, Esmerelda." The man said.

"Selena?" She turned to look at the other woman next to her.

"It's true. The Goddess chooses whom you bind your soul to. If she chooses to mate a powerful witch and an alpha wolf, then there's a reason."

"How do you know I'm an alpha?"

"Well, you're not yet but you will be."

I nodded. "How do you know that?"

"I just know things," The one they called Selena shrugs nonchalantly.

"You marked her already?" The other one named Esmerelda asked as she looked at her sister's neck and shook her head. "I didn't think you had that in you, Marie."

Marie looked down at the ground embarrassedly. I squeezed her hand.

"It's different when you find your mate."

"Your parents won't be okay with this." The blonde man interjected.

"They'll have to be, Drake," Selena stated. "You can't remove a mark."

"You'll come to our home tomorrow for dinner." Esmerelda instructed.

Marie's sisters didn't seem to object to our mating, but I couldn't ignore the skepticism in Drake's voice. I knew he was right; my own pack wouldn't accept a witch as their alpha's mate. But I couldn't help the way I felt about Marie, the way she completed me in ways no other wolf ever could. I looked down at her, still holding her hand tightly, and knew that I would fight tooth and nail for us to be together.

The rest of the night, we stayed close to each other. Marie introduced me to more of her witch coven, and they all welcomed me warmly. I could sense their magic swirling around us, and it made me feel alive in a way that I never had before.

As the night drew to a close, Marie's sisters made their way to us. "We'll see you tomorrow," Esmerelda said, smiling at me. "Don't be late."

I kissed Marie goodbye and watched as she climbed into a jeep with Drake and her sisters.

"You found your mate?" Matias asked as he joined me in the parking lot.

I nodded. "Slight problem though."

He cocked an eyebrow. "She's not a wolf."

"How do you know?"

"I could tell instantly," He laughed. "Your father is not going to accept this."

"I know," I sighed.

Marie

The next morning, I walked down to the kitchen where my parents and sisters were already mulling about for breakfast.

"What is that smell?" My father asked. He turned around and pinned me with a stare. "Why do you smell like a werewolf?"

"I...uh...I..." I stammered. "I met my mate last night."

"We are witches we don't have mates; we have eternal heartlines."

"I met my person last night," I replied confidently as I raised my chin.

My father narrowed his eyes and looked at me. "What coven is he from?"

"He's a werewolf."

My father broke out into laughter. My facial expression didn't change, and he narrowed his eyes again.

"You're serious? I forbid this. You can't mate with a wolf. It's impossible."

"Nothing is impossible if the Moon Goddess has declared it so." Esmerelda interjects.

"The Moon Goddess?" My father scoffed. "Marie doesn't know what she's talking about. She just fell for some dog's lines."

"He obviously knew, daddy," Selena added. "He marked her. A wolf isn't going to mark a random girl."

"What?" My father bellowed. The lights began flickering and there was a loud popping noise.

"I forbid this."

"He's coming to dinner tonight. Why can't you just give him a chance?" I asked.

"He's not coming to dinner."

"You'll be able to tell if he's lying. If his intentions are pure."

My father crossed his arms over his chest and narrowed his eyes at me. "You think I'll just let some mutt into our home for dinner? Absolutely not. You're young and naive, Marie. You don't understand the dangers of getting involved with a werewolf. They're wild, unpredictable creatures. It's in their nature to hunt, to kill. They'll never be able to control their instincts. It's only a matter of time before he turns on you."

I rolled my eyes. "That's just a bunch of stereotypes, Daddy. He's not like that. He's kind, gentle, and caring. He protected me last night."

"And what makes you think he won't turn on you? Or worse, what if his pack finds out about you? They'll tear you apart, Marie. Is that what you want?"

I sighed, knowing that arguing with my father was pointless. He was stubborn and set in his ways. But I wasn't going to back down on this.

"This isn't some random guy I met, and think is cute. It's more than that. If Grandpa had told you that you couldn't date Mom, what would you have done?"

"Dated me anyway, because that's what happened." My mother giggled.

My father hesitated for a moment before letting out a resigned sigh. "Fine, he can come to dinner. But if he steps out of line, I won't hesitate to take action."

I let out a sigh of relief and hugged my father. "Thank you so much. You have no idea how much this means to me."

As the day went on, I couldn't help but feel nervous. What if my father was right? What if this was all a mistake? But as soon as I saw him, all my doubts vanished.

"Andrei," I breathed. He pulled me into a hug and a hungry kiss. My body melted into his.

We pulled away and he placed his forehead against mine for just a second before he looked toward the man standing next to him.

"This is my best friend, Matias." Andrei introduced a tall, muscular man with dark hair and brown eyes to the group.

"Hi, Matias. Welcome to our home." I smiled.

Dinner was tense at first, but as we began to talk, the atmosphere lightened up.

My father was still a jerk throughout most of the meal, but it seemed as though he was coming around.

"Would you like to take a walk?" I asked Andrei. "My sisters can entertain Matias."

He smiled, his eyes flitting to Matias who nodded at him.

He laced his fingers through mine. My spine tingled as a jolt of electricity rushed through me.

Andrei

A s soon as we were away from the house, I pulled her into a kiss.
"I've been wanting to do that all night."

"I know. I felt your hunger."

I kissed her again. The moon was full and bright, and the air was cool and crisp. Andrei took my hand and led me to a secluded corner of the garden.

"I know your father doesn't approve of us," he said softly. "But I can't stay away from you."

"I feel it too."

"We have to treat this delicately. I don't...I don't believe my pack will accept us."

"What do we do then?"

"I'm trying to figure that out. I'm not losing you though."

She leaned into me. I wrapped my arms around her and held her tightly.

"I'm not losing you either."

"I have to get back to the compound. We have training early tomorrow."

She nodded and leaned up on her tiptoes to kiss me.

As we parted ways, I couldn't help but feel a sense of longing within me. I knew the risks of being together, but I also knew that I couldn't live without her. I needed her to breathe, to live, to exist.

As I walked towards the compound, my mind wandered to our last encounter. I replayed the moment over and over again in my head, remembering the way her lips felt against mine, the way her body molded into mine, and the scent of her that lingered on my clothes.

But as I entered the compound, reality hit me like a ton of bricks. I pulled out my cell phone and called my mother.

"Andrei, it's so good to hear your voice." My mother greeted me on the other end.

"Yours too, mama," I smiled.

"What's wrong, baby?"

"Mama," I began to argue and protest that nothing was wrong, but she knew me better than that. "I found my mate."

"That's amazing. I'm so happy for you." She inhaled sharply. "Uh oh. What's wrong?"

"She's not a wolf. She's a powerful witch."

"A witch," She gasped. "Goddess, what have you done?"

"I love her, I don't know what to do."

"She's your mate child, it doesn't matter what anyone else says. If the Goddess made it happen there's a reason."

"Papa will not agree."

"I won't argue that." She sighed. "Keep this to yourself for now. I will take care of Papa."

"Yes ma'am."

We talked about Marie for a little while before I hung up the phone and went to my bunk.

I didn't know what the future held as far as my pack and my family were concerned. I would give them all up for Marie in a second.

As I drifted off to sleep, I knew that I would have to face the consequences of my actions soon enough. But for that moment, I allowed myself to indulge in the memory of the taste, of her lips, and the warmth of her embrace.

The next morning, I woke up to the sound of my alarm clock blaring. I rubbed my eyes and sat up in my bunk, feeling more tired than I had ever been. The training was grueling, but I forced myself to push through it.

As I stood in the sparring ring with my fellow pack members, I couldn't stop thinking about Marie. It was as if she was always there with me, even when she wasn't.

After training, I went to my mom's place. She was waiting for me outside of her house, her arms open wide. I ran towards her and hugged her tightly, feeling the weight of my worries lift off my shoulders.

"Your father is not happy," she whispered.

"I expected as much," I replied. "But I can't help how I feel. Marie is my mate. I can't just abandon her."

"I know that, and I support you. But there will be consequences. The pack won't accept her easily, and some may even try to cause her or her family harm."

"I can handle it," I said, more confidently than I felt.

"I know you can. But you don't have to go through it alone. I'll be here for you, always."

"Thank you, mama. That means a lot."

When I finally arrived at my bunk, I collapsed onto my bed and closed my eyes. I needed rest, both physically and emotionally.

Marie

As I stood in front of the mirror, adjusting the last few strands of my brown hair, I couldn't help but feel a mixture of excitement and nervousness.

It had been a week since I'd last seen Andrei. He wasn't allowed to leave the compound except for one night each week.

Tonight was our first date. I had always prided myself on being a powerful witch, but with him, I felt vulnerable in the most enchanting way.

I smoothed out my emerald-green dress and took a deep breath, reminding myself to be confident. Pushing those butterflies aside, I headed downstairs to where Andrei was waiting.

As I descended the stairs, my heart skipped a beat at the sight of him. He was tall and rugged, with a magnetic aura that drew me in. His eyes, a mesmerizing shade of green, met mine, and a slow, charming smile spread across his lips.

"You look absolutely stunning," he said in that deep, velvety voice that sent shivers down my spine.

I felt a blush creep up my cheeks as I replied, "Thank you, Andrei. You clean up pretty nicely yourself."

He chuckled, his eyes never leaving mine. "Shall we?"

Offering my arm, he guided me to the door with a confidence that matched his appearance. We stepped out into the cool evening air, the moon casting a silvery glow on everything around us. His hand brushed against mine, sending a jolt of electricity through my veins. I suppressed a gasp, not wanting to reveal just how much he affected me.

We walked to his truck and got in, our conversation flowing effortlessly. We spoke about our lives, our experiences, and our dreams.

His laughter was like music to my ears, and I found myself opening up in ways I hadn't expected. It was as if we had known each other for a lifetime.

As we approached a cozy little restaurant tucked away in a corner, Andrei held the door open for me. The warm ambiance of the place welcomed us, and the scent of delicious food wafted through the air.

Over dinner, our conversation deepened, and I was struck by how much we had in common. We both loved the outdoors, had a passion for helping those in need, and shared a fondness for classic literature. His eyes sparkled with genuine interest as I talked about my magical practices, and I could tell that he respected my abilities.

"You know, there's something incredibly captivating about the way you talk about magic," he said, his voice a mixture of awe and admiration.

I smiled, feeling a warmth spread through my chest. "Andrei, you have a way of making me feel truly seen and understood."

He reached across the table, his fingers brushing against mine, and a tingle of energy passed between us. "I feel the same way, Marie. It's like we're connected on a level that goes beyond words."

As the evening wore on, I found myself lost in his stories and anecdotes, hanging onto his every word. And he seemed just as engrossed in my tales of battling dark forces and uncovering ancient spells. It was as if our souls were dancing together, weaving a bond that was unbreakable.

"I want to get you into my truck and kiss you for the next few hours."

"Then ask for the check so we can go," I smiled. He chuckled, nodded, and did as he was told.

Twenty minutes later, we were in the back seat of his truck on a dark deserted road. He lay me down and kissed his way from my mouth, down; his fingers playing in my slick folds.

My body shivered, and I let out a soft cry. My fingers dug into his shoulder as I bit my bottom lip. I pulled him closer, my fingers tangling in his hair. He kissed the inside of my thighs.

"Andrei," I moaned his name. His lips moved higher, and I felt his tongue. My back arched as much as I could with him atop me, and I called out again.

"Please," I begged him.

He growled and reached for his zipper. He freed his cock, and I slid my hand in between us. I found his length and stroked him gently. He gasped, and his mouth came down, his tongue flicking against my clit. I'd never been with someone so attentive before. My hips rocked, and I moaned and called out his name again. He reached up and pulled my hand down.

That's when I realized how strong he was. I gasped, and he flicked his tongue over my slick folds before he teased me with that same little bit of pressure against my clit.

"Yes" I whimpered. My fingers tightened in his hair, and I tilted my hips. He curled his fingers around my hips, holding me in place.

His tongue teased me some more, and my heart pounded. "Please," I whispered. He took his finger and put it inside me. I moaned as he curled it and pressed against my G spot. I arched my back and called out his name.

"Fuck," I groaned.

My hand grabbed the back of his head, and he slid his fingers out of me. Without hesitation, he put the head of his cock against my entrance.

"Are you sure?" he asked, and I nodded.

I was so wet that he slid inside me with ease. My nails bit into his shoulder, and he gasped. Slowly, he slid out and pressed in again. He kept his movements slow, but I needed more. "I need you to fuck me hard and fast," I said, and he groaned.

Fire shot through my veins. His teeth grazed my ear. "I want to hear you scream," he whispered. His teeth pulled against my earlobe, and my body jerked. He chuckled softly and pressed his hips down on mine. I cried out, and his fingers bit into my hips. He started to move faster, and I groaned. The heat inside me burned, and I felt myself getting higher. He pushed in deeper, and his thumb brushed over my clit. My body shivered, and my back arched.

"Oh Goddess, Andrei," I whispered. My hands slid over his back, and I dug my nails in.

His pace quickened. He pulled out almost all the way before he slammed back in. His cock hit my G spot each time, and my vision started to go black.

"Harder," I moaned.

He pumped his hips harder, and he cried out. I knew he was close. I wanted to feel him come inside me. My back arched, and my hands dug into his shoulders.

"Fuck, Marie," he growled.

My heart pounded as he slammed into me harder and harder. The heat inside me spread, and I called out his name. He growled and kissed my lips. My tongue slid over his, and I moaned into his mouth as my body quivered beneath him.

A moment later, I felt him shudder. He thrust inside me a few more times before he cried out my name. He buried his face in the crook of my neck and breathed heavily. This was the last thing I wanted to do right now. I just wanted to curl up and sleep with him, but he pulled out of me and got up. We got dressed, and he pulled me against his chest.

"I have to get back to the compound."

"I know," I murmured.

"I only have two weeks left and then we can be together every day."

I smiled at him as I lay my head on his chest.

"I can't wait."

Andrei

"Andrei," Marie stood before me two weeks later in her front yard. She took my hands in hers. "I'm pregnant."

"Marie, how is that...I didn't think it was possible."

"I didn't either. I took a test. I went to the doctor. I'm pregnant"

"Have you told anyone?"

"My sisters know. They're willing to help us hide if we need to."

"We can't..." I inhaled and exhaled. "I have to go to my father. If...if anyone finds out that you're carrying a hybrid child then..."

"I know."

My phone began ringing. I looked down to see my father's number come across the screen.

"I need you home now." He growled into the other end. "Papa," I began.

"You need to leave the witch behind and come back to Missouri. The council has learned and they're summoning you."

"I'm not leaving her papa."

"Don't be stupid. I can't protect you if you don't."

"She's carrying my child."

"She's what?" My father's growl echoed through the phone.

There was a rustling noise behind me, I turned to see a red mangey-looking mutt come out of the bushes.

"Papa, now is not the time."

"Is there someone there?"

"Yes, Papa."

"Is Matias with you?"

"No, Papa."

He let out a slew of curse words before he hung up the phone.

"Andrei," Marie breathed as she took a step toward me. I stepped in front of her.

"They're here for her," Indrik growled. *"They know."*

"I am aware. How many are there?"

"He's a decoy. There's at least ten nearby."

I inhaled and searched the mind link for Matias.

"I need you."

"I'm already on my way," Matias replied.

"My sisters are close by," Marie told me through our link. I nodded my head.

I morphed into my jet-black wolf. Marie gasped but she kept her spot beside me, stroking my fur as she did.

The red wolf lunged, and I did the same.

Our jaws locked together as we tumbled across the ground, growls and snarls echoing throughout the clearing. I could hear the sounds of the other wolves approaching, their footsteps pounding against the earth.

Marie stood her ground, her hands balled into fists as she watched the fight unfold. I could feel her fear, her anxiety, and her love for me pulsing through our link.

She roared behind me, the Latin flowing from her lips, and her hands crackled with lightning, arcs of energy leaping from her fingers as she spoke spells of protection and power over herself.

I managed to break free from the red wolf's hold and lunged forward, but he dodged my attack and countered with one of his own. His teeth sank into my shoulder, and I let out a yelp of pain.

Suddenly, there was a blur of fur as Matias appeared on the scene. He tackled the red wolf, taking him by surprise and sending him sprawling across the ground. With his attention diverted, I took advantage of the situation and lunged forward once more.

Selena and Esmerelda appeared, the three women were battling the wolves with us as they wove their hands in intricate spells and threw our enemies without touching them.

My jaws clamped down on the red wolf's neck, and I felt his body go limp beneath me. I released him and turned to survey the area. The other wolves had been taken care of by Marie, her sisters, and Matias. We had won.

Marie came up to me, her hands shaking as she reached out to touch my fur.

"Andrei, you're hurt," she said, tears in her eyes. I nuzzled her hand gently, reassuring her that I was fine.

Matias came up to us, his eyes scanning the area. "We need to go. More could show up any minute now."

I took one last look at Marie before I shifted back into my human form.

"We have to leave," I said, grabbing her hand and pulling her with us. She nodded.

"Our parents have transportation waiting for you." Esmerelda interjected.

She was shaking, tears rolled down her cheeks as she hugged her sister.

"You're not coming?" Marie asked.

"We will be here making plans. We will arrive soon." Selena murmured as she hugged Marie tightly.

Tears rolled down all their cheeks. My heart was breaking.

"We have to go," Matias growled.

"Get in the car," Marie's father hissed at us. "Now."

Matias climbed in the driver's seat with an address that Marie's father had given him. Marie and I climbed in the backseat.

She leaned into me and sobbed into my chest.

"Your father will meet us here. I sent him the address through our link." Matias explained as he looked at me in the rearview mirror. We finally reached a small cabin in the woods. It was run down and abandoned, but it would have to do for now.

Marie collapsed onto the couch, exhausted and scared. I sat down beside her, taking her hand in mine.

"We'll figure this out," I said, trying to reassure her. "

"Is this what our life will be forever?" She asked.

"I don't know," I answered. She fell asleep, crying quietly sometime later.

The next morning, I awoke to a knock on the door before my parents walked into the cabin.

My father's two top men followed behind him. They walked around the cabin, securing it. My mother rushed to hug me and Marie.

"You have marked her, no?"

"Yes sir."

"I've spoken to the council; we will perform the ceremony and she will become a member of our pack."

"The pack..."

"Will accept you, your mate, and your child if I say so. I've gotten the council's approval." "Thank you, Papa." "You two, and your unborn child won't survive a day out here if you're not protected by the pack." "I know," I murmured.

"What about my family?"

"I've spoken with your parents." Matias interjected. "They agree."

"We will leave now to go home. Your family will meet us there for the ceremony."

And just like that, without a choice or argument we loaded into my parent's SUV, with a security detail, and headed back to Missouri.

Marie didn't speak. She just held my hand tightly.

We were about to start our life together whether we were ready or not.

Marie

I held onto Andrei's hand like the lifeline that it was. I was terrified but I knew protecting the child growing inside me was the most important thing right now.

Andrei was my mate and I wanted to be with him forever; whatever it took for that to happen.

When we finally arrived in Missouri, we were greeted with open arms by the pack members.

My parents and sisters were also there waiting for us.

"The Alpha has given us permission to come and go as we please." My father smiled. "This is the best thing for you three." "I know daddy. I've never been away from y'all, though." "I know, baby," He chuckled as he pulled me into a hug. "It's time to be an adult. You'll have a family of your own soon."

"Yes sir," I nodded.

The ceremony was held in a small clearing in the woods, surrounded by the pack members. I wore a white dress that flowed around me, my hair pulled back into a bun. Andrei stood beside me, dressed in a white shirt and black pants. Our parents stood behind us, their hands on our shoulders.

As the ceremony began, my stomach began to growl.

"I'm hungry, but I didn't want to get anything on my dress." I giggled.

Andrei smiled back at me. He took my hands in his.

"Don't worry love, I'll take care of you," he whispered before placing a kiss on my forehead.

The ceremony was brief but beautiful. As we exchanged our vows, I couldn't help but think about the life growing inside me. I placed a hand on my belly, feeling the slightest flutter.

After the vows were exchanged, we celebrated with a feast. The pack members had hunted and prepared a feast fit for royalty. I sat at the head of the table with Andrei by my side, feeling overwhelmed by the love and support of our pack.

As the night wore on, our celebration turned into a wild party. The music was loud, the drinks were flowing, and everyone was dancing. Andrei pulled me onto the dance floor, holding me close as we moved to the beat.

In that moment, nothing else mattered. The fear and uncertainty of the past few weeks were forgotten, replaced by the love and joy of our union.

But as the night wore on, my hunger returned with a vengeance. I tried to ignore it, but it was impossible. I needed to eat before I passed out.

"I need to sit down," I said to Andrei, my hand on my stomach.

He looked at me with concern before nodding. "Let's go get you some food."

We made our way over to the table, where there was still plenty of food left. I loaded up my plate, not caring about the stains on my dress anymore. I was too hungry to care.

He whispered in my ear, "Come on love, let's go somewhere more private."

He led me to a small cabin in the woods, away from the noise of the party. As soon as we were inside, he kicked the door shut and pulled me into his arms. His lips met mine in a fiery kiss, igniting a passion inside me that I had never known before.

He pressed me against the wall, his hands exploring my body as I clung to him. I felt a hunger inside me that was not just for food. I wanted him, all of him.

"Andrei," I gasped as his lips trailed down my neck. "I need you."

He didn't need any more encouragement. He lifted me up and carried me to the small bed in the corner of the room. We fell onto it in a tangle of limbs, our breathing ragged with desire.

As he stripped off my dress, I felt a primal urge to do the same for him. I wanted to see his body, feel it against me. I ripped his shirt open, sending buttons flying across the room. I pulled it off over his head, gasping at his muscular chest and abs.

I pulled him down on top of me as my hands explored his chest, feeling his muscles ripple under my hands. I arched my back, pressing my body against his as his lips found mine again. His hand trailed down my body, slipping inside my panties. I gasped as his fingers found my clit, rubbing it slowly.

"Please Andrei," I whimpered, my body craving more.

He slipped off his pants, throwing them to the floor. He climbed back on top of me, kissing me again as his cock pressed against my entrance.

I let out a moan as he thrust inside of me, our bodies moving together.

"Yes," I moaned as his cock slid in and out of my tight pussy, his lips pressed against my neck.

I wrapped my legs around him, pulling him in deeper. I could feel an orgasm building inside me as his cock rubbed against my G-spot. My hips bucked against him, my back arching off the bed.

I cried out as the orgasm hit, my pussy throbbing around his cock. He grunted, thrusting harder as the pleasure washed over me. As the orgasm subsided, I moaned, knowing there was more to come.

He pulled out of me, flipping me over onto my knees. I felt him enter me from behind, thrusting hard into my dripping pussy.

"Fuck," he growled, his hands gripping my hips as he slammed into me.

"Oh yes," I moaned as his cock hit my G-spot again.

"You like that?" Andrei's voice was husky.

"Yes!" I moaned in response.

He pounded into me, my cries growing louder. I could feel another orgasm approaching. I arched my back, my pussy tightening around his cock.

With a grunt, he came inside me, his hot cum filling me. I cried out as the orgasm washed over me, my pussy throbbing as I came.

"Fuck," I breathed, my body exhausted.

Andrei pulled out of me, collapsing next to me on the bed. I rested my head on his chest, my fingers tracing patterns on his muscular arms. I could feel his heart beating, the heat of his body pressed against mine.

We did not get much sleep that night, but I was not complaining.

"Andrei, I'm starving." I murmured as I rolled out of the bed.

"It seems I forgot to stock the cabin with food," He chuckled. "We can go to the pack house and eat. It's breakfast time."

We got dressed and made our way to the pack house. We walked in and immediately I was hit with all the breakfast smells. The kitchen was set up like a breakfast buffet.

As I ate, I noticed a strange feeling in my stomach. It was like the baby was kicking, but it felt different than it had before. It was stronger, almost painful.

"Andrei," I gasped, dropping my fork. "Something's wrong."

He was by my side in an instant, his hand on my back. "What is it? What's wrong?"

"The baby," I said, tears forming in my eyes. "It hurts."

He lifted me into his arms, carrying me to a nearby couch. He rested me on it, his hands on my stomach.

My mother was standing before me as was his mother.

"Andrei, take her upstairs to the bedroom. It's time."

"Time? What do you mean?" I gasped.

"It's time to deliver this baby," My mother giggled.

"That's impossible."

"You're a witch carrying a werewolf's baby," My mother laughed. "Nothing is impossible at this point."

My eyes were wide with terror as I looked back at Andrei. He picked me up and carried me into a bedroom like he'd been instructed. He carefully placed me on a bed, holding my hand the entire time.

I had barely gotten used to the fact that I was growing a child, a hybrid child at that, inside of me and here I am about to deliver the baby and be a mother.

Andrei

We were about to be parents. I would spend the rest of my life protecting this woman and our soon to be born child.

As we sat in the room, I couldn't help but feel a sense of overwhelming love and protectiveness wash over me. My hand never left hers as she squeezed it tightly, riding out the waves of pain that came with each contraction.

I watched as her face contorted in pain and I felt a surge of guilt. I was the one who put her in this position, the one who couldn't control my urges. But now, as I watched her struggle, I knew that I would do anything to make this right.

I leaned in and whispered words of encouragement, telling her how strong she was and how proud I was of her. She squeezed my hand harder, her eyes locked on mine as if to say "I need you here with me."

Hours passed and finally, we heard the sound of our baby's cry. I watched as the doctor placed our little one in her arms and tears streamed down her face. I couldn't help but feel overwhelmed with emotion as I looked at the new life that we had created together. The weight of responsibility hit me like a ton of bricks.

As our baby girl settled into her mother's arms, I knew that I would do anything to protect her. To be the father that she would need in this crazy world. I vowed to always be there for her, to support her dreams, and to teach her to be strong and independent like her mother.

"Well, it looks like we have a new granddaughter." My mother grinned from ear to ear. "She's precious."

"She's so beautiful." Marie's mother breathed. "

She looks so much like you, Marie."

"What's her name?"

"Eva," Marie breathed.

"That's beautiful." I sighed.

"How do...how do we know if she's a wolf or a witch?" Marie asked softly.

Her mother giggled as she reached over and stroked her daughter's hair. "She's both, sweetheart. She's both parts of you, I'm sure."

"How can she be both?"

"You'll see."

The room fell silent as we all stared at Eva, taking in her tiny features and wondering about her mysterious heritage. I couldn't help but feel a sense of awe as I thought about the power and potential that she held inside.

As if sensing our thoughts, Eva opened her eyes and gazed up at us with a calm, knowing expression. It was then that I realized that she was different from any other child I had ever seen. She was special.

Over the next few weeks, Marie and I settled into our new roles as parents, learning the ins and outs of taking care of a newborn. But there was something else that we had to learn as well - how to help our daughter navigate the strange world that she had been born into.

"Andrei!" I heard Marie scream shrilly.

I raced to Eva's room, where the scream had come from.

"What's wrong?"

"Eva's missing."

"What?" I gasped. I looked into her crib, and she was no longer there. My stomach dropped.

We began looking around as if she could have crawled out or something.

I heard a whimper coming from the closet. I flung open the door to find a silver wolf pup inside. Her bright blue eyes looked up at me sadly.

I picked her up and chuckled.

"I think I found her."

"That's a...oh my Goddess." Marie gasped as she put her hand over her mouth. "She shouldn't be able to do that yet."

I shook my head. "Looks like she's definitely got a wolf in her."

Eva's mixed heritage meant that she had powers that we couldn't even begin to comprehend.

Most wolves aren't able to transition until after their sixteenth birthday, Eva was changing at just six days old. There was no rhyme or reason to it either, but we'd mostly find her like that after a nap or in the middle of the night.

That wasn't her only power though. We watched in amazement as she levitated objects and teleported them across the room. But even as we marveled at her abilities, we knew that we had to protect her. There were those who would seek to harm her for being different, and we couldn't let that happen.

We kept her powers a secret from day one, to protect her.

"ANDREI," MARIE CALLED as she and Eva played in the living room.

"Yes, my love?" I replied as I walked in to see two pieces of my heart smiling back at me.

"Eva has something for you." Marie stood Eva up and helped her walk toward me. She was wearing a shirt that said I'm the big sister.

"Marie? You're pregnant?"

"Yes," She giggled. "Get ready for chaos, the doctor says it's twins."

I nearly passed out. I grabbed her in a hug and kissed her passionately.

Our lives had been altered so quickly and continued to change daily. Eva was our miracle and now we'd be bringing two more into the world. At least, Eva wouldn't have to weather the storm of being different alone.

"Chaos coordinator, at your service." I replied with a wink. "Bring it on, we can get through anything together, baby."

Don't miss out!

Visit the website below and you can sign up to receive emails whenever Luna Rains publishes a new book. There's no charge and no obligation.

https://books2read.com/r/B-A-VUJHB-QQPBD

Connecting independent readers to independent writers.

Did you love *Fated Mate Surprise Daddy*? Then you should read *Fated Mate Triplets Daddy* by Luna Rains!

Every heartbeat screams her name, demanding my action; I am her protector, her savior, her fated mate.

Threatened by a supernatural enemy, we cross paths.

The chemistry of our bond is clear and the physical craving can't be denied.

Then, the unthinkable happens. She is abducted by the mad vampire that has been chasing me for years.

My werewolf rage and need to protect her are ignited within me.

With each step, I'm plunged deeper into the treacherous world of paranormal creatures, desperate to rescue the woman I can't live without.

But the stakes are higher than I ever imagined because she's carrying my triplets.

Read more at https://lunarains.com.

Also by Luna Rains

Fated Mates Saga
Fated Mate Surprise Daddy
Fated Mate Triplets Daddy

Watch for more at https://lunarains.com.

About the Author

I am Luna Rains, a romance author raised amid the enchanting allure of the southern landscape. My roots are deeply entwined in the mysteries of the South, and my novels exude an irresistible blend of paranormal fascination and scorching passion.

Hailing from a small Georgia town, my upbringing amidst ancient oaks and whispered legends fueled my imagination. Savannah, my hometown, is known as the most haunted city in the country. Now in my thriving thirties, I channel my intrigue for the unknown into spellbinding tales of ethereal love. My novels entwine spectral beings with unbridled desire, painting a world where love defies both time and the supernatural.

With a devoted following, I have mastered the art of kindling flames through my paranormal romance stories, etching my name as a maestro of the genre. My passion for crafting tales that blend the mystical with the sensual has become my signature, and I take pride in transporting my readers to realms where love knows no bounds.

Read more at https://lunarains.com.

www.ingramcontent.com/pod-product-compliance
Lightning Source LLC
Chambersburg PA
CBHW031138160726
47987CB00026B/1440